An Irish Night
Before Christmas

An Irish Night Before Christmas

By Sarah Kirwan Blazek
Illustrated by James Rice

PELICAN PUBLISHING COMPANY
Gretna 1996

*With much love to my mother, my son, Beau,
and my husband, Frank,*

*and with a special word of appreciation to my editor,
Nina Kooij*

First printing, April 1995
Second printing, March 1996

*The word "Pelican" and the depiction of a pelican are trademarks
of Pelican Publishing Company, Inc.,
and are registered in the U.S. Patent and Trademark Office.*

Library of Congress Cataloging-in-Publication Data

Blazek, Sarah Kirwan.
  An Irish night before Christmas / by Sarah Kirwan Blazek ;
illustrated by James Rice.
      p.   cm.
  Summary: An adaptation of the famous poem about a Christmas Eve
visitor, set in Ireland.
  ISBN 1-56554-086-7
  1. Christmas—Ireland—Juvenile poetry. 2. Santa Claus—Juvenile
poetry. 3. Children's poetry, American. [1. Christmas—Poetry.
2. Santa Claus—Poetry. 3. Ireland—Poetry. 4. Narrative poetry.
5. American poetry.] I. Rice, James, 1934- ill. II. Title.
PS3552.L398I75 1995
811'.54—dc20   94-42911
                                                                          CIP
                                                                          AC

Printed in Hong Kong
Published by Pelican Publishing Company, Inc.
1101 Monroe Street, Gretna, Louisiana 70053

AN IRISH NIGHT BEFORE CHRISTMAS

'Twas the night before Christmas
And down the glen lane
The candles they twinkled
In each windowpane.

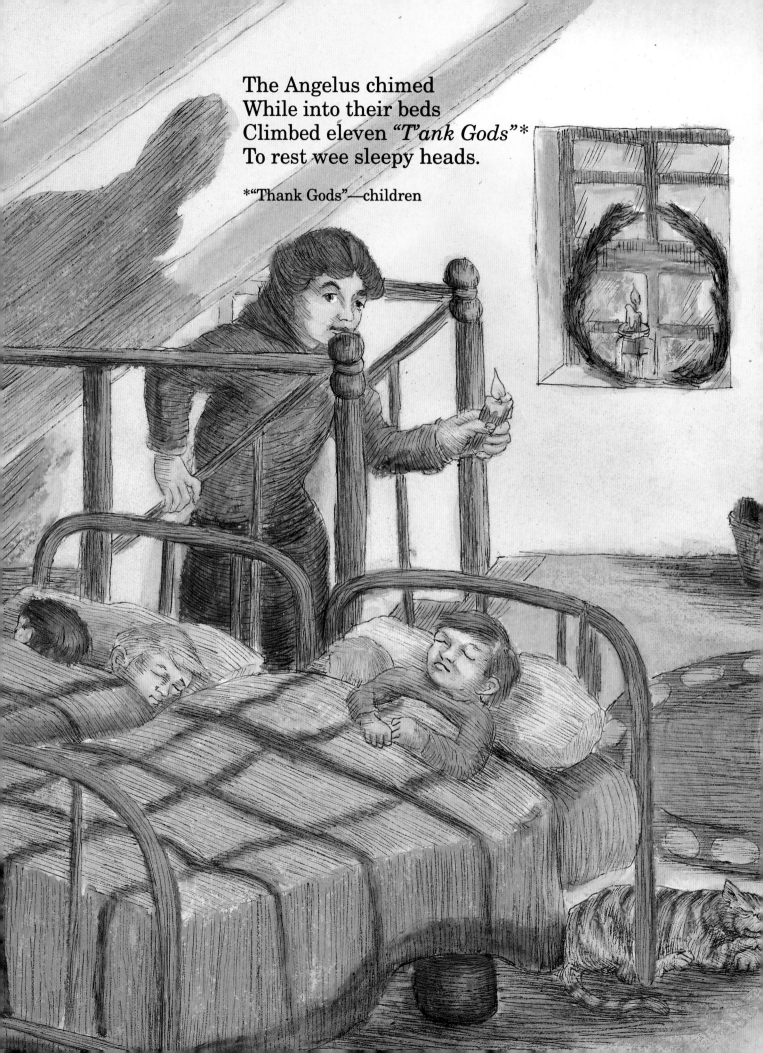

The Angelus chimed
While into their beds
Climbed eleven *"T'ank Gods"**
To rest wee sleepy heads.

*"Thank Gods"—children

Herself shut the latch
On the ould wooden door.
Meself piled turf
On the hearth once more.

"Arrah musha," says she.
"I'll make me some tea."
"Ay and make some for me,
Cushla machree."*

*Darling

"Don't tell that to me,
Ould Paddy Magee.
It's stout that you're after
When you're not after me!"

"Arrah," says I,
"God forgimme. What matter?
But sure, begorra,
What is that, that clatter?"

The moon as if laughing
Played tricks on the stones.
They smiled out like jewels
From green fields and roads.

Wisha, God help me,
In front of me eyes—
A donkey and cart,
Sailing clear through the skies!

I wouldn't be joking;
I saw them meself.
I rubbed me ould eyes—
Out jumped a wee elf.

No sooner I turned,
By the good saints in Heaven—
Out jumped not one
But a magical seven!

As cute as the devil,
In Aran and green,
Stood ould Father Christmas,
Looking ever so keen.

He shouted out orders:
"To the top of the thatch.
Slide down the chimney—
Throw open the latch!"

"Up Sean, up Patrick,
Up Kevin and Kerry.
Up Colum and Cormac,
Up Angus; don't tarry."

As quiet as church mice
They bounced on the floor.
Those wee ones, so clever,
They opened the door.

Father Christmas he entered
So full of good cheer;
Irish eyes twinkling,
Whispered, "God save all here."

His hair, it was wirey,
His beard soft as down—
A robust old bucko,
Face freckled and round.

In one hand, his blackthorn,*
And over his back
Were crackers and treasures
In a well-worn sack.

*Shillelagh

He eyed the plum pudding,
The loveliest scene.
He laughed to himself
As he spied the poteen.*

*Whiskey

"The dampness it bothers
Me ould tired back.
I'll have one small sup
While I unload my sack."

The wee ones they giggled
And scampered about,
Filling up stockings
And sipping the stout.

The time passed so quickly
With laughing and fun.
It wasn't so long;
The work was all done.

When all of a sudden
A table was tipped.
Plum pudding and trifle
Lazily dripped.

"We'll be on our way, boys,"
Said ould Father Christmas.
Just then came a noise
And out came the missus.

The wee ones and Santa
Finished their stout.
Down the stair came herself
Shouting, "Out, rascals, out!"

Ould Neddy the donkey
With unshod hoof
Was happily waiting
While eating the roof.

They jumped in the cart,
Not a moment to spare.
Down the glen lane
Their cart it did tear.

For it's ne'er a Christmas
When everything's right,
But with the wind at our backs
The world's looking bright.

Father Christmas exclaimed,
For wherever we roam,
"Nollaig sona agut!*
There is no place like home."

*Merry Christmas to you